D0516146

COUNT YOUR CHICKENS

JO ELLEN BOGART
LORI JOY SMITH

TUNDRA BOOKS

FLOWERS

RESTAURANT

PIES

TOWN

Chickens, chickens everywhere
going to the county fair.
Turn the page to join the fun —
count some chickens! Start with one.

THE SEA

FUN SLIDE

THE FAIR

COTTON CANDY

Picky chickens choose the best —
find their favorites, leave the rest.
Chickens paint their fancy toes,
listen to their radios.

Chicken grannies knitting socks.
Chicken chicks with chicken pox.

Chickens ready for the day.
All is done — they're on their way!

Chicken pilots flying planes.
Chicken engineers on trains.

Chicken farmer shows his plant.
Chicken racers puff and pant.
Chicken chefs and pastry cooks,
chickens watch with hungry looks.

Chicken princess throws a ball.

Slapstick chicken takes a fall.

Chicken clowns in floppy shoes.

Moody chickens sing the blues.

Chicken doctors treat the sick.
Slick magicians do a trick.

Chicken punks with funky feathers
strut their stuff in studded leathers.

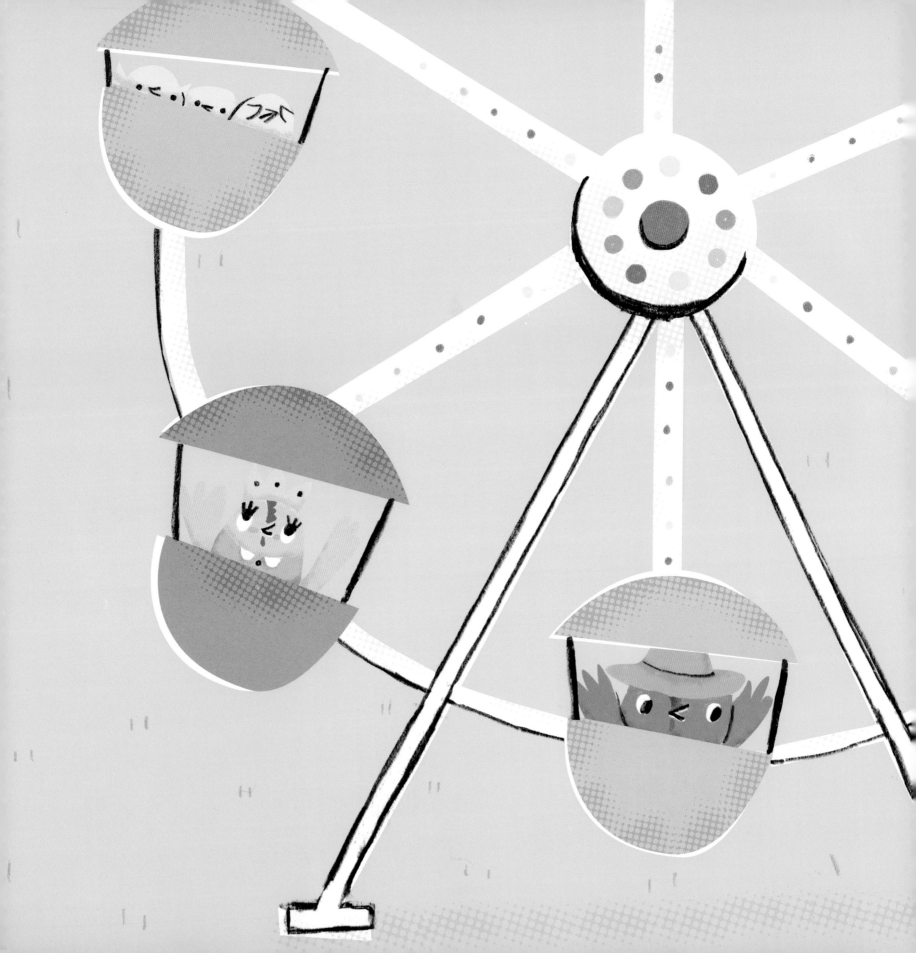

Chickens on the Ferris wheel
shriek with laughter, scream and squeal.
Chicken sister cannot speak —
cotton candy in her beak!

Chickens on the super slide
have a super thrilling ride.

THE DIXIE CHICKI

Banjo chickens pluck and pick.
On the strings, these chicks are quick.

Chickens in pink underpants
love the music, have to dance.

COTTON CANDY

"What a show!" the chickens roar,
stamp their feet and yell, "Encore!"

COUNTY FAIR

Show is over, lights go down.
Chickens heading back to town.
Mama chicken had such fun,
tells her chicks, "It's late, we're done."

Little chickens, overfed,
carried home and put to bed.

Chickens, chickens everywhere
had a great time at the fair.

1. How many chickens are sitting on the stoop?

2. How many chickens are knitting?

3. How many chickens are on the train?

4. How many chickens are in the sack race?

5. How many chickens are holding balloons?

6. How many chicken clowns are there?

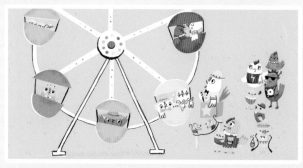

7. How many chickens are under the tent?

8. How many chickens are riding the Ferris wheel?

9. How many chickens are going down the slide?

10. How many chickens are on stage for the big show?

11. How many chickens are wearing sunglasses?

12. How many chickens are riding skateboards?

13. How many chickens are tucked into bed?

Turn the page to find out if you've counted your chickens right!

To my wonderful grandchildren – Milo, Esme, Astrid and Teagan.
— JEB

For my mom and dad, for always loving this crazy chicken!
— LJS

Text copyright © 2017 by Jo Ellen Bogart
Illustrations copyright © 2017 by Lori Joy Smith

Tundra Books, a division of Random House of Canada Limited, a Penguin Random House Company

LIBRARY AND ARCHIVES CANADA CATALOGUING IN PUBLICATION

Bogart, Jo Ellen, 1945–, author
     Count your chickens / by Jo Ellen Bogart ; illustrated by Lori Joy Smith.

Issued in print and electronic formats.
ISBN 978-1-77049-792-4 (bound). – ISBN 978-1-77049-794-8 (epub)

     I. Smith, Lori Joy, 1973–, illustrator II. Title.

PS8553.O465C68 2017   jC813'.54   C2015-901060-8
                                        C2015-901061-6

Published simultaneously in the United States of America by Tundra Books of Northern New York,
a division of Random House of Canada Limited, a Penguin Random House Company

Library of Congress Control Number: 2016933060

Edited by Sylvia Chan and Jessica Burgess
Designed by Five Seventeen
The artwork in this book was rendered in pencil and colored digitally.
The text was set in Aunt Mildred.
Printed and bound in China

www.penguinrandomhouse.ca

1 2 3   4 5   21 20 19 18 17

Penguin
Random
House
TUNDRA BOOKS

ANSWER KEY

How Many?
1. 3
2. 2
3. 7
4. 5
5. 3
6. 3
7. 8
8. 10
9. 7
10. 4
11. 4
12. 2
13. 3